LADY

LOLLIPOP

ISBN 0-439-40129-1

12 11 10 9 8 7 6 5 4 3   2 3 4 5 6 7/0

Printed in the U.S.A.   40

First Scholastic printing, January 2002

This book was typeset in Stempel Schneidler and Gararond.

The illustrations were done in pencil.

LADY
LOLLIPOP

Dick King-Smith

illustrated by Jill Barton

SCHOLASTIC INC.
New York Toronto London Auckland Sydney
Mexico City New Delhi Hong Kong Buenos Aires

CONTENTS

Was there ever such a spoiled child?

CHAPTER ONE

Once upon a time,
in a faraway land,
there lived a little
princess. She was seven
years old, soon to be eight, with short brown hair and
large brown eyes, and she was a very spoiled child.

Her mother, Queen Ethelwynne, spoiled her quite a
bit, but her father, King Theophilus, spoiled her rotten.

So that all the courtiers at the Royal Palace, and all the servants too, from the Lord High Chamberlain to the smallest scullery boy, agreed among themselves that little Princess Penelope was a right pain in the neck.

As her eighth birthday approached, the King and Queen were discussing what they should buy their beloved only child as a present.

"What about a pony, Eth?" said the King.

"I don't think she likes horses very much, Theo," the Queen replied. "How about a puppy?"

"She's never been too keen on dogs," said the King.

"Well, a kitten then?"

"Or cats," said the King.

"Well then, let's ask her what she would like," said the Queen.

"But then it won't be a surprise. Still, I expect you're right. Let's have her in and see what she says."

So they sent a servant to summon the Princess, and waited.

And waited.

"She can have absolutely anything she likes, of course," said the King.

"Well, I don't know . . ." began the Queen.

"Absolutely anything," said the King.

Shortly the servant returned with a message from Princess Penelope that she would come when she was ready and not before.

King Theophilus laughed.

"She's got a will of her own, has our Penelope," he said.

"You can say that again," said the Queen.

Just then the door burst open and in came the little Princess with a face like thunder.

"What d'you want?" she said. "You interrupted a game I was playing."

"Now, now," said the Queen, and "Steady on, old girl," said the King. "We want to ask you something. What would you like for a present on your eighth birthday? A pony?"

"Don't like horses," said the Princess.

"A puppy then?" asked the Queen.

"Don't like dogs."

"Or a kitten?"

"Or cats."

14

"Well, you tell us, darling," said King Theophilus. "What *would* you like?"

"A pig," said the Princess.

"What!"

"I want a pig for a pet."

"A pig, Penelope?" cried the Queen. "But a pig is a dirty animal."

"Is not!" said the Princess.

"A pig," said the King, "is an ugly beast."

"Is not!!" shouted the Princess.

"A pig," said the King and Queen with one voice, "is a stupid creature."

"Is not!!!" yelled the Princess at the top of her voice.

"I wanna pig,

I wanna pig,

I wanna pig!"

So loudly did she yell that everyone in the Royal Palace heard her, from the Lord High Chamberlain to the smallest scullery boy, and everyone thought, Was there ever such a spoiled child?

Queen Ethelwynne looked at her husband.

" 'She can have absolutely anything.' That's what you said, Theo," she remarked.

King Theophilus sighed.

"All right then, my sweet," he said. "Daddy will buy you a pig."

A bit of a strange name

CHAPTER TWO

The first thing that the King
did was to issue a Royal
Proclamation, which stated
that every pig keeper in the kingdom was
commanded to bring one pig to the Palace at a certain
time on the day of Princess Penelope's eighth birthday.

"That way, Eth," said the King to the Queen, "our
Penelope will have the widest possible choice."

So, when the time came, dozens and dozens of pig
keepers gathered in the Great Park, in the center of
which the Palace stood.

Each man had brought one pig, in a cart or on a rope or,
if small enough, in his arms, and what a selection there
was. There were big pigs and middle-sized pigs and little

pigs, there were pigs with upright ears or droopy ears, with long snouts or pushed-in faces, and as for color, why, there were pigs of every imaginable hue. Many were whitish of course, but some were black, some reddish, some striped, some spotted, all lined up on the green grass of the Great Park, ready for the Princess's inspection.

Most of the pig keepers knew that the Princess was a very spoiled child, and many of them expected that she would not be satisfied with just one pig. The King and the Queen rather expected this too, and they kept their fingers crossed as they walked along the lines behind the birthday girl.

But, far from choosing lots, the Princess passed from pig to pig and all she said was "No."

"Do you like this one, Penelope darling?" the King would say.

"No."

"Or this one perhaps?" the Queen would say.

"No!"

But after a bit they gave up asking because "No!" became "NO!!"

"I'll tell you when I find the one I want," said the little Princess. "Just stop nagging me."

Each pig keeper was of course very disappointed as

the inspection party passed him by, for to have had his pig chosen to live at Court would have been the greatest honor.

But it was beginning to look as though the Princess simply couldn't find anything she liked. Whatever the size or shape or color, she merely scowled and shook her head and marched on.

Until there was only one animal left, at the very end of the very last of the lines of pigs of all sorts.

This last pig, the King and Queen could see, was quite different from all the other fat, well-groomed animals. They say that pig keepers tend to look rather like their charges, and most of the owners were, if not well groomed, on the fat side. But the last pig was a long skinny creature, held on the end of a piece of string by a long skinny boy. It was a dirty white in color and the boy looked none too clean.

Princess Penelope pointed at this last pig.

"Want *that* one," she said.

"But darling," said the King, "you can't have that one. It's the scruffiest, ugliest pig of the lot."

"Is *not*!" shouted the Princess, and she folded her arms and scowled furiously at her father.

Now all the pig keepers in the Great Park fell silent and so even did their pigs. Everyone waited to see who would win this battle — the King, monarch of all he surveyed, or his spoiled little daughter.

But before either could say a further word, to everyone's surprise, the last pig's owner spoke.

"You're right, miss," said the boy to the Princess. "You've picked the best one. Scruffy and ugly she may be, like your dad says, but she's the brightest, cleverest pig you ever did see. Just watch this."

Then he said to his pig **"Sit"**

and she sat,

and **"Down"**

and she lay down,

and **"Roll over"**

and she rolled over,

and **"Stand"**

and she stood up again, looking

up at the boy and waiting for the next command.

"Will you look at that!" said the other pig keepers in astonishment, while their pigs voiced their amazement in a flurry of grunting.

"I trained her myself," said the long skinny boy, and he handed the end of the string to the Princess. He swallowed, as though there was a lump in his throat.

"I shall be ever so sorry to see her go," he said. "She's all I've got."

"You must have a mother and father, haven't you?" said the Queen.

"No, I'm an orphan."

"Oh well, don't worry," said Princess Penelope. "Daddy will get you another pig," and she took hold of the animal's string and said "Sit."

The pig remained standing.

The Princess stamped her foot.

"SIT!" she shouted again, but nothing happened.

"Choose another pig, Penelope, my love," said King Theophilus. "This creature only obeys the boy."

To everyone's surprise, the Princess did not shout and yell at this. Instead she stood, hands on hips, facing her father, and said in a very quiet voice, "I . . . want . . . this . . . pig."

"Oh," said the King. "Sorry," he said to the boy, "she wants *your* pig."

"Could I come and see her now and again?" the boy said. "The pig, I mean?"

He turned to the Princess.

"Could I, miss, please?"

Now, as this oddly assorted couple of children faced one another — the Princess in a new, expensive party frock, the boy, half a head taller, in his torn and dirty clothes — something quite unexpected happened.

The Princess smiled.

Whether it was because she felt some pity for the boy, or whether she'd worked out that he'd be useful for jobs like mucking out the pig, or whether it was because the pig suddenly sat down before her and looked up into her eyes and gave a little grunt, no one knew. But those nearest saw her smiling, first at the pig and then at the ragged boy.

"What's your name?" she said.

"Johnny, miss. Johnny Skinner."

"All right, Johnny Skinner," said Princess Penelope. "You can be my personal pig keeper. You can go on looking after this pig, which is now *my* pig, my birthday pig. Understood?"

"Yes, miss," said Johnny.

"But darling . . ." began the Queen.

"But Penelope . . ." began the King.

"But nothing," said the Princess. "Come on, Johnny."

And back they marched along the lines, the Princess with her birthday present, then Johnny Skinner, then King Theophilus, and then Queen Ethelwynne.

"By the way," said the Princess over her shoulder to her new pig keeper, "what's her name, this pig of mine?"

"Well, miss," said Johnny, "it's a bit of a strange name really, but it's what I've always called her."

"What is it?"

"Lollipop."

I wonder if I could train her?

CHAPTER THREE

"I like it," said the Princess. "It's a nice name. But why is she so thin? Don't you feed her properly?"

"I've no money to buy food for her," said Johnny Skinner.

"What's she been eating then?"

"Whatever she could find on the rubbish heaps, miss."

"We'll have to do something about that," said the Princess.

When they reached the Palace gates, she stopped and turned to face her father.

"Daddy," she said.

"Yes, darling?"

"I want . . ." and she went through a whole list of things she wanted done.

"Yes, certainly, my love," said the King.

So that by the end of the day, no one who had seen her that morning in the Great Park would have recognized the pig called Lollipop. She had been washed and scrubbed and groomed and oiled, and she lay in a deep bed of clean straw in one of the stalls in the Royal Mews, her stomach filled with a lovely mess of rich scraps from the Royal table and leftovers from the Royal kitchens.

By her side sat a very different-looking boy, for Johnny Skinner had taken a proper bath (for the first time in his life), and his old clothes had all been burned. Fitted out in new ones, his stomach also comfortably full, he got to his feet as the door of the stall opened and in came Princess Penelope, carrying a birthday cake with eight candles on it.

"Here we are, Johnny," she said. "I had to give a bit each to Daddy and Mommy, but the rest is ours," and she cut three big slices.

"Thanks, miss," said Johnny, and Lollipop grunted.

Though the boy could not know it, a bit of a change had come over the birthday girl. Because of her rank and because of her spoiled and often sulky nature, she had never had any real friends. Now she was beginning to feel she had one.

"You shouldn't really call me 'miss,' Johnny," she said.

"Why not, miss?"

"Because you should address me as 'Your Royal Highness.'"

"Oh."

"But actually I don't mind. Have some more cake."

So he did, and she did, and so did the pig, till there was nothing left but the eight candles, and then Lollipop ate them too.

Princess Penelope stroked her pig.

"Sit!" she said, but the pig remained standing.

The Princess pouted.

"Why won't she do what I tell her?" she said. "Everyone else does what I tell them. Why won't my pig?"

"It's early days, miss," said Johnny. "She's only ever been used to me."

"Well, she's not yours any longer," said the Princess sharply, "and don't you forget it." And out she flounced.

"Don't you worry," said Johnny to Lollipop. "I shall always think of you as mine," and he rubbed behind her ears, something she specially liked, so that she gave little soft squeaks of pleasure.

"They were right," went on Johnny. "She is a spoiled child. But in a way it's not her fault. It's the fault of her dad and mom for letting her have everything she wants. She was quite nice, wasn't she, when we were eating the cake, don't you think?"

Lollipop grunted.

"But then the moment she couldn't get her own way, she flew off the handle, didn't she?"

Lollipop grunted again.

"I've been quite successful at training you," Johnny Skinner said to the pig. "I wonder if I could train her?"

He might have felt doubtful if he could have witnessed

the scene in the Palace that evening.

"Bedtime, Penelope," said the Queen.

"No," said the Princess.

"Tell her, Theo," said the Queen.

"Come on now, Penelope old girl," said the King. "You've had a long day. You must be tired."

"Am *not*. I don't want to go to bed yet. It's my birthday."

"Yes," said the Queen, "and you've had lots of presents, including a very special one from Daddy. Not many little girls get a pig for a birthday present, and by the way, I haven't heard you thanking him yet. How about saying 'Thank you, Daddy' now?"

"Shan't. Not unless you let me stay up late."

"She could, couldn't she, Eth?" said the King. "Just this once? Just for a treat?"

"Oh, I wash my hands of it!" cried the Queen, and she went to arrange some Royal roses in a Royal rose bowl.

"Till midnight, Daddy?" said the Princess.

"Well, all right then," said the King. "Just this once."

The Princess smiled a self-satisfied smile.

"Thanks," she said. "For the pig, I mean."

"I'm glad you like it, darling," said the King. "I'm sure it's very comfortable in its stall."

"Oh, you needn't think it's going to stay there forever."

"What do you mean?" said the Queen, looking up from her roses.

"My pig," said Princess Penelope, "is going to be a house pig. Or I suppose I should say, a palace pig."

And then all the members of the Royal household, from the Lord High Chamberlain to the smallest scullery boy, heard Queen Ethelwynne go off into screaming hysterics.

Busy! Understand?

CHAPTER FOUR

One thing you could say for certain about that spoiled child Princess Penelope — she didn't mess around.

Hardly had the grooms and stable lads begun work in the Royal Mews next morning than the Princess appeared, making for the stall in which her pig was kept.

Johnny Skinner had just returned from the Royal kitchens with a bucketful of tasty pig swill, and Lollipop was tucking in, snout deep in the trough.

"Johnny," said the Princess. "You think yourself a brilliant pig trainer,

don't you? You could train Lollipop to do anything, I suppose?"

"Well, I don't know about that, miss," said Johnny. "I could train her to do most things, I suppose."

"But could you train her *not* to do *some* things?"

"How d'you mean, miss?"

"Could you train her not to do things in the house? Could you house-train her?"

"Well, she's never lived in a house."

"But she's going to live in one now," said the Princess. "In fact she's going to live in the Palace, my pig is. So could you palace-train her?"

For a moment Johnny did not answer. He stood scratching his head and wondering if it would be possible.

Princess Penelope stamped her foot.

"Well?" she said. "Could you or couldn't you?"

With a pig as intelligent as Lollipop, Johnny thought, I reckon I could.

"I reckon I could, miss," he said, "but she'll have to stay in this stall for a while yet, and then if she makes any mistakes, it won't matter. It'll take a bit of time."

"Well, don't waste any then," said the Princess sharply. "Get on with it." And off she went.

Thoughtfully, Johnny Skinner scratched Lollipop's bristly back, a back that seemed already to be getting plumper than it had been.

"What d'you think, old girl?" he said to her as she licked the last of her breakfast from the trough. "Do you think you could learn to be palace-trained?"

Lollipop grunted. To Johnny's ears, Lollipop had a whole vocabulary of different grunts that all, he was sure, meant different things:

like **"Scratch my back"**

or **"Rub my ears"**

or (mostly) **"I'm hungry."**

But there were two
distinct grunts
that Johnny
knew meant

"Yes"   or   **"No."**

"Yes" was a quick, slightly high-pitched grunt. "No" was a deeper grunt, more long-drawn-out.

Now, in answer to Johnny's question, Lollipop clearly gave the "Yes" grunt.

"Right," said Johnny. "Then we'll give it a try. But if you're going to finish up palace-trained, you'll have to begin by becoming stall-trained," and he tied the old bit of rope around the pig's neck and opened the door into the yard outside.

First, thought Johnny, I must teach her a new word of command that she will learn to understand, just as she does with "Sit" or "Down."

He looked at Lollipop and saw that she was gazing up at him with bright, intelligent eyes, just as though she were aware of the thoughts that were going through his head, and suddenly he knew the word he was going to use.

He took the rope off her neck, pointed to a patch of grass on the far side of the yard, and said to the pig "Busy!"

Lollipop looked up at him again, then looked across the yard.

"Busy!" said Johnny again. "Understand?"

And Lollipop gave the quick, high-pitched grunt, trotted over to the patch of grass, and did everything that Johnny wanted her to do.

I'll jolly well make you a duke

CHAPTER FIVE

Poor King Theophilus! He
found himself between a rock
and a hard place.

On one side was his
daughter, quite determined
that her new pet should be a
palace pig.

On the other, his wife, who,
after her bout of hysterics
upon learning of this, had
served upon him the
following ultimatum.

"If that ugly, dirty, stupid
animal sets trotter inside these

walls, Theo," the Queen had said, "then out I go. There isn't room for both of us."

"But my dear Eth," said the King, "we have two hundred and forty rooms in this Palace."

"Which," replied the Queen, "is not going to be turned into a pigsty."

Next morning, meeting his daughter as she returned from the Royal Mews, the King said to her, "You were joking, weren't you, Penelope? About your new pet, I mean. I forget its name."

"Lollipop."

"About Lollipop becoming a palace pig? It was just a joke, wasn't it?"

"No," said the Princess.

"But," said the King, "your mother does not wish it."

"Well I do, Daddy."

"But . . . but . . . but," said the King, "it'll make messes everywhere."

"No, it won't," said the Princess. "I am having it palace-trained."

"By that boy, d'you mean? I forget his name."

"Johnny Skinner. I have just given him orders about it. Lollipop should soon be able to leave the stall and live with us."

"But Penelope," said the King, "if she does, your mother has said she will leave us."

"You must tell her not to, then," said the Princess Penelope. "After all, Daddy, your word is law."

She smiled sweetly.

"I always do everything you tell me, don't I?" she said.

King Theophilus took a deep breath.

"Well, darling," he said, "I am telling you now — you cannot bring that pig into the Palace."

He waited nervously for the outburst that must surely follow. Would she go into a terrible sulk? Would she shout and yell at him? Would she throw things?

Once, in a fury, she had kicked his shins. He drew back a pace or two.

But to his surprise the Princess only gave him another sweet smile.

"Didn't you hear what I said?" asked the King.

"Yes," said the Princess, "but I'm not going to take a blind bit of notice of it," and off she went.

The King shut himself in his study.

"What am I to do?" he said out loud. "Why must the child be so unreasonable?

Who is there who might make her see sense? Wait though! What about that boy? Suppose I told him I didn't want the pig to be palace-trained? He'd be bound to do what I told him, wouldn't he?"

So he sent for Johnny Skinner.

Johnny of course had never been inside the Palace before, and now, as he followed the footman who had brought the message to the Mews, he looked around him in wonder at all the rich furnishings, at the ornaments of gold and silver, at the portraits of the King's ancestors looking down at him from the tapestried walls, and felt beneath his feet the thick softness of the priceless carpets upon which, if all went well, Lollipop would before long be walking.

"Come in! Come in!" cried the King in a hearty voice when the footman opened the door. "Sit down, Johnny my boy. Make yourself comfortable. How are you? Well, I hope?"

"Yes, sir," said Johnny.

"And your pig?"

"She's well, sir," said Johnny, "but she's not my pig anymore."

"No, of course not, quite so," said the King. "But though you're no longer her owner, you are nevertheless her trainer, are you not?"

"Yes."

"You teach her things, don't you?"

"Yes, sir," replied Johnny. "I'm teaching her something new now."

"What?"

"I'm house-training her."

"Palace-training, you mean?" said the King.

"Yes."

"Are you telling me that you'll be able to teach her never to . . . er . . . um . . . never to do anything indoors?"

"Yes, sir."

"Like a well-trained dog, you mean?"

Johnny nodded.

If he really can do that, thought the King, then Eth won't have anything to complain about. Maybe Penelope will get her own way, after all. Like she always does.

"Johnny," said the King. "Tell me honestly. Would you say that my daughter is a bit spoiled?"

"No."

"Oh. What would you say then?"

"That she is very spoiled indeed. She needs to be taught to think more about other people and less about herself."

Dead right, thought the King.

"Could you teach her, d'you think?" he said.

"I might be able to."

"If you can, Johnny," said King Theophilus, "I'll jolly well make you a duke."

You always want to get your own way

CHAPTER SIX

A duke, thought Johnny
as he left the Palace.
Duke of what? Duke Skinner sounds a bit funny. Still, it
would have to be a good thing. I mean, dukes don't live
in stalls, do they? So I'd better work hard on this
training business — not only training the pig (which I
think will be fairly easy) but also training the Princess
(which I'm sure will be pretty difficult).

Back in the stall, he sat down beside Lollipop and said to her, "What do you think? Could I train that girl to be less selfish and spoiled?"

The pig gave her "Yes" grunt.

"But how shall I start?" said Johnny.

At that very moment, in came Princess Penelope.

Johnny stood up and said to the pig "Stand," and the pig stood up.

The Princess looked around the floor of the stall.

"The straw seems to be very clean," she said. "Have you just mucked out?"

"No, miss," said Johnny. "No need for that, you just watch." And he opened the door and called Lollipop out and said "Busy!"

The Princess watched, amazed, as the pig trotted across the yard to the patch of grass and performed perfectly.

"That's brilliant, Johnny!" the Princess said, and when the pig came back, she too said to her "Busy!"

The pig gave a deep, long-drawn-out grunt.

"No good saying that now, miss," said Johnny. "She's only just done it."

"Well then, sit!" said the Princess to the pig. Lollipop remained standing.

"*Why* won't she do what I tell her?" said Princess Penelope angrily. "Stupid animal!"

The Princess didn't notice, but Lollipop was watching her carefully. The pig put her head on one side as though she was listening to these words, and she fluttered her long white eyelashes. Johnny felt that if she'd had eyebrows, she would have raised them in surprise.

At that moment, he had an idea. "Look, miss," he said, "Lollipop isn't stupid. She just hasn't been trained to obey you, only me. But I might be able to train her to obey you too, if you would do something for me in return."

"Like what?"

"Well, to begin with, you could speak more politely to Lollipop," said Johnny (and to me, he thought).

"Animals are very sensitive to the tone of people's voices. Try talking to her more gently, if you want her to obey you."

He knelt down in the straw on the far side of Lollipop and began to rub behind her ears.

"Now try telling her to sit again, miss," he said, and he ducked his head down behind the pig's.

Then, the moment that the Princess said "Sit" (in a more kindly voice), Johnny whispered the word into one of the pig's ears, and down she sat.

"She did it!" cried Princess Penelope. "I told her to do it and she did it! What shall I tell her to do next, Johnny?"

Johnny Skinner stood up, brushing bits of straw off his knees.

"That's enough to begin with, miss," he said.

"Is *not*!" cried the Princess, stamping her foot. "I want to make her do other things. Stand, Lollipop. *Stand! Will* you do what I say!" But the pig remained sitting, at the same time giving the "No" grunt in answer.

"Stand," said Johnny quietly, and she stood up.

Just as quietly, he said to the Princess, "You've got to learn to be more patient, you know, if you want your pig to obey you. No good shouting at her and losing your temper. Trouble with you is, you always want to get your own way."

This is the moment, he said to himself. If she acts now like the spoiled little madam she is, then I'm never going to be able to do anything with her and she'll never mend her manners. And I'll never be a duke, what's more!

Johnny stood, the pig at his side, waiting for the outburst.

Opposite him, the Princess stood with a face like thunder.

Then, in the silence, Lollipop moved forward and came to stand before the Princess, gazing up into her face with bright eyes. The Princess, staring into those eyes, fringed with long white lashes and shining with intelligence, saw someone not so very different from herself looking back at her.

At that moment, though she herself did not realize it, Princess Penelope grew up a little bit.

She looked at Johnny Skinner, and Johnny smiled at her.

"All right, Johnny," she said. "I'll try to be more patient. With both of you."

"Good," said Johnny. "That's good, miss. Isn't it, Lollipop?" And the pig gave that quick, high-pitched grunt.

What a good girl!

CHAPTER SEVEN

"The next thing to do," said Johnny to Lollipop once the Princess had gone, "is for me to teach you to obey her. I shan't be able to get away with whispering in your ear every time. I've never used food rewards with you before but I think this is the time to start," and he begged a small sack of horse biscuits from one of the stable lads in the Mews.

When the Princess next visited the stall, Johnny explained his plan to her.

"First, tell Lollipop to sit," he said, "which you're going to do in a nice voice, aren't you?"

The Princess nodded.

"And then," said Johnny, "if she doesn't obey you, simply turn your back on her. But if she does obey you, then give her a few biscuits and a lot of praise. Understand, miss?"

The Princess nodded.

So Johnny passed her a handful of the biscuits, which she pocketed.

Then he in turn nodded directly at her.

Before them Lollipop stood, her eyes fixed on the girl. She had seen the handful of biscuits — she could smell them, she wanted them.

"Sit, Lollipop," said Princess
Penelope in a quiet voice.

The pig remained
standing.

The Princess turned
her back on her pet.

Lollipop looked up at Johnny.
It was an enquiring look,
a what-have-I-done-wrong look.

Johnny said nothing, but merely frowned and shook his head at the pig.

"Turn around again now, miss," he said, "and try again."

The Princess turned.

"Sit," she said quietly once more.

Lollipop shot a glance at Johnny and saw that he was both smiling and nodding. She saw also that the Princess's hand had gone to her pocket.

The pig sat down.

"*What* a good pig!" cried the Princess, and she held out some biscuits on the palm of her hand.

Lollipop took the biscuits quite delicately, at the same time giving out a string of contented little grunts. Johnny, who understood her language pretty well, was fairly certain that she was saying, "Hey! This girl's not so bad after all. The boy has never rewarded me with food, but the girl is going to if I do what she tells me."

And so when the Princess said "Stand," the pig stood up and got some more biscuits and a lot more praise.

"What command shall I try next, Johnny?" said the Princess, again in a quiet voice.

"I think we'd better just stick to S–I–T and S–T–A–N–D for the moment, miss," replied Johnny. "I'm spelling them," he said, "so as not to muddle her. Try another S–I–T."

So the Princess did, and the pig obeyed immediately. Reward and praise followed, as they did after Lollipop just as promptly stood again when told.

After half a dozen sits and stands, Johnny said, "I think that's enough for today. We don't want her to get bored. She's done very well."

"What about *me*, Johnny?" said the Princess with just a touch of her old petulance.

"You've done well too, miss. Very well."

"Anyone would think you were training me!" laughed the Princess. "I'm surprised you didn't say, '*What* a good girl!' and offer me some horse biscuits. When can I have my next lesson, Mr. Skinner, sir?"

"Tomorrow, miss," Johnny said.

"I wish you'd stop calling me 'miss,'" said the Princess.

"But you said you didn't mind."

"I don't, but why can't you call me by my name?"

"Call you Penelope, d'you mean?"

"Yes," said the Princess. "Think about it. See you tomorrow."

Johnny thought about it. If I do call her Penelope, he said to himself, she'll maybe get angry and bite my head off. Likewise if I don't. Can't win.

But then something told him that he would be silly not to do as the Princess asked. It was beginning to look as though she wasn't such a bad sort of girl after all.

If the pig comes in, Mommy goes out

CHAPTER EIGHT

"Daddy," said the Princess
that evening.

"Yes, my love?"
replied King Theophilus.

"It won't be long now before Lollipop can come and
live in the Palace."

The King looked nervously around in case Queen
Ethelwynne should have heard these words, but she
was not in the room.

"Oh, Penelope darling," said the King, "you can't do
this. I told you, didn't I? If the pig comes in, Mommy
goes out."

He waited, even more nervously, for the explosion that always followed if his daughter's wishes were thwarted.

To his surprise, the Princess replied, "Look Daddy, I promise you that my Lollipop will be perfectly palace trained. Mommy has no need to worry."

What's come over her, thought the King. Why is she speaking in such a reasonable way?

"Johnny Skinner is training her to be a perfect palace pig," said the Princess, "and what's more, he's training me too."

"Training you?"

"Yes, to be a bit more patient and not to shout and lose my temper. He said I always want to get my own way."

"Did he indeed?" said the King.

He remembered what Johnny had said to him — "She needs to be taught to think more about other people and less about herself."

"Penelope darling," he said. "I do hope that you will change your mind about bringing your pig into the Palace, however well-trained it becomes."

The Princess smiled.

"No, Daddy dear, I shan't change my mind," she said. "You'll just have to change Mommy's."

That evening, the King tried.

"Eth dear," he said. "About Penelope's pig . . ."

"What about Penelope's pig?" said the Queen in a dangerously quiet voice. "Don't imagine for one moment, Theophilus, that you can persuade me to change my mind and allow that ugly, dirty, stupid animal into my Palace."

"But . . ." said the King.

"No buts," said the Queen. "I'm going to bed. Good night."

To begin with, it was not a good night for the King as he tossed and turned beneath the tufted tester of the great Royal four-poster bed, unable to sleep. His thoughts ran around and around the same track. Penelope was going to bring the pig into the Palace. Then Eth would leave it. What a scandal there would be throughout the kingdom! Everyone, from the Lord High Chamberlain to the smallest scullery boy, would know that Queen Ethelwynne had upped and left King Theophilus. And why? Because the King had allowed the Princess Penelope to bring her pet pig to live in the Palace.

Half the populace would say, "And I don't blame the Queen!" and the other half would blame him, saying, "What sort of a king is he if he can't control his own little daughter?"

The fact is, nobody can control her, thought the King wearily, lying and listening to the Queen's soft snores. But then, toward dawn, it suddenly occurred to him that there was somebody who could control her! Johnny Skinner!

Very carefully, so as not to wake the Queen, King Theophilus got out of bed.

Like all people who work with animals, the grooms and stable lads in the Royal Mews began their duties very early in the day. It was barely light when, to their great surprise, they saw entering the mews the figure of the King, in a robe and nightshirt and slippers, on the Royal head not a crown but a tasseled nightcap.

All took care to pretend to be unaware of his presence, but out of the corners of their eyes they saw him enter the stall in which the Princess's pig was kept.

Inside, the pig lay in the straw alone, for Johnny had already left to collect all last night's scraps from the Royal kitchens.

As the King came in, the pig stood up. A gesture of respect, the King thought, though in fact Lollipop had supposed it was Johnny, coming with her breakfast.

I must say, thought the King, she looks twice the pig she was.

"Good morning, Lollipop," he said. "I trust you are well?" He was answered by a quick, high-pitched grunt from the pig, who stood before him, gazing up into his face with bright eyes.

The King, staring into those eyes, fringed with long white lashes and shining with intelligence, saw someone not so very different from himself looking back. The pig, it seemed to the King, even fluttered her eyelashes at him.

Just then Johnny came in with the swill bucket, and Lollipop let out a loud squeal, the meaning of which was plain even to the King.

"Excuse me, sir," said Johnny. "Can't keep her ladyship waiting," and he sloshed the food into the trough.

Her ladyship, thought the King, as he watched the pig tucking in. If the boy can find a way out of the mess I'm in, I'll not only make him a duke, I'll award her the title of Lady Lollipop.

"How's the training going, Johnny?" he asked.

"I'll show you, sir," said Johnny, "just as soon as she's finished," and when she had, he opened the door, called her out and told her to be busy.

"See, sir?" said Johnny as they watched. "No problem. She could move into the Palace tomorrow."

Wipe your feet

CHAPTER NINE

"Amazing!" said the King. "But still, she'd bring a lot of muck in on her feet, wouldn't she? Mud all over the carpets, I mean?"

"I'd thought of that, sir," said Johnny, and he produced a large doormat that he laid down in front of the pig.

"Wipe your feet," he told her, and at these words Lollipop walked forward and scraped first her front trotters and then the back ones on the mat.

"Astonishing!" said the King. "But then how's she going to get out when she wants to? There may not always be someone to open the door for her, like you just did."

"I'd thought of that too," said Johnny, and he unrolled a scroll of paper upon which he had drawn a diagram. It was a picture of a door, an ordinary door, except that in the middle of the lower half of it there was a pig-sized section that had been cut out and hinged at its top, to swing either way.

"It's a pig flap, d'you see?" said Johnny. "When Lollipop wants to go out, she'll push with her snout at the bottom of the flap and it'll swing open and through she'll go, and she'll come back in the same way. She'll be independent."

"Astounding!" said the King.

"You have a door leading to the Royal Gardens, sir, I suppose?" asked Johnny.

"Oh, yes."

"The Palace carpenters could soon put a pig flap in

that, working from my design. Then you'd have nothing to worry about, sir. Lollipop goes into the garden when she needs to and wipes her feet when she comes back in."

"Oh, but Johnny," said the King, "the Royal Gardens are the Queen's pride and joy. She doesn't much like digging, you know, too much like hard work, but she especially loves her rose garden. Roses are her favorite flowers and she's never happier than when she's picking them or pruning them or deadheading them. Just think of the damage that pig could do in the Royal Gardens!"

"An ordinary pig, yes, sir," said Johnny. "I quite agree. But just think of the good that a very intelligent, highly trained pig like Lollipop could do. At one end she could turn over the soil in the flower borders and plough up the vegetable patch with her snout, and at the other end — well, pig dung is very good for roses, sir. It would be easy for me to teach Lollipop to be busy in the rose garden. You never know, she might become quite popular with the Queen, and then —"

"And then," interrupted the King, "she might be allowed into the Palace! Johnny, you're a genius!"

He looked at Lollipop, who was still snuffling around her trough in case she'd missed anything, and then he said, "Gosh! I'm hungry! Have you had your breakfast, Johnny?"

"No, sir," replied Johnny.

"Well, come back home with me and we'll all have breakfast together."

By now it was broad daylight, of course, and there were plenty of people about to see the King, in robe and nightshirt and slippers, on his head not a crown but a tasseled nightcap, walking back to the Palace in earnest conversation with the boy who looked after Princess Penelope's pig.

"I feel like having my favorite breakfast," the King was saying to Johnny. "Scrambled eggs on fried bread. Does that sound all right to you?"

"It certainly does," said Johnny.

Back in the Palace, they found the Queen and the Princess at the breakfast table.

"You remember Johnny, Eth?" said the King.

"I do," said the Queen. "Though it is something of a surprise to see him here."

You wait, thought the King, you may be getting a bigger surprise before long, and he gave orders for the two breakfasts — "As quick as you can, we're starving."

"Are you not going to dress, Theo?" asked the Queen.

"Later, my dear, later. Now then Johnny, sit down. Sit beside Penelope there."

Johnny sat down, opposite the Queen, who, he could see, was looking very disapprovingly at him over a

great bowl of roses that stood in the middle of the table. He leaned across to sniff at them.

"My favorite flowers," he said.

The Queen's expression softened a little.

"But," said Johnny, "never in my life have I seen such beautiful ones. Please ma'am," he said to the Queen, "what variety are they?"

The beginnings of a smile appeared on the Queen's face. "They are a new hybrid," she said, "grown

especially for me. In fact they are called Ethelwynne's Beautiful."

"How true, ma'am," said Johnny, and the Queen inclined her head, smiling broadly now.

"So you like roses, do you?" she said.

"Oh yes, ma'am," said Johnny. "I would love to see your rose garden."

"Get this lot down you first, Johnny," said the King as two huge platefuls appeared, "and then I'm sure the

Queen will show you around afterward, won't you, Eth?"

The Queen, her own breakfast finished, stood up.

"Come and find me when you're ready, boy," she said, and she left the room.

"Just what's going on, Daddy?" asked the Princess. "What have you been up to, wandering around in your nightclothes? Have you and Johnny been hatching some plan?"

"We have," they both replied, and they told her about the doormat and the pig flap, and the scheme for making Lollipop useful in the Royal Gardens, so that hopefully the Queen would come around to the idea of her becoming a palace pig.

"Things are looking good, Penelope," the King said. "It looks as though Mommy's already taken quite a shine to Johnny. The next step is to make her like his pig."

"*My* pig, Daddy!" said the Princess sharply.

"Sorry, sorry, your pig, darling," said the King hastily.

He too now got up from the table, rubbing his tummy appreciatively, and went out of the room.

Johnny swallowed his last mouthful.

"That was lovely, miss," he said.

"*Not* 'miss,' Johnny, remember?"

Perhaps because he was so pleasantly full of scrambled eggs and fried bread Johnny replied, easily and naturally, "Oh sorry, Penelope."

The Princess smiled.

"Come on, I'll show you the way to Mommy's rose garden," she said.

She's got a nice smile, Johnny Skinner thought as he followed.

She had better come in to tea

CHAPTER TEN

That night, as the King and the Queen lay side by side beneath the tufted tester of the great Royal four-poster bed, the Queen said, "You know, Theo, that boy Johnny knows a lot about roses."

"Does he indeed, Eth?" said the King.

"Yes, he knows all the different types, the hybrid teas, the floribundas, the climbers, the ramblers, and which months they flower in and which ones are resistant to disease. He's not just a swineherd, he's a bright boy."

"Good, good," said the King. "Did he talk to you at all about Lollipop?"

"I presume you mean that pig."

"Yes."

"Certainly not. The boy has sense enough to know that I do not approve of the creature."

There was a longish silence, during which the King considered the idea of having a proper row with the Queen about Penelope's pig. After all, I am the King, he thought. Everyone has to do what I tell them. Even the Queen. But, he said to himself, if we do have a row about it, I know who'll win, and it won't be me.

Just then the Queen said sleepily, "I might find a job for that boy in the garden."

"Good, good," said the King.

The Queen yawned.

"Good night, Theo," she said.

"Good night, Eth."

After a few minutes the Queen said, "I've been meaning to ask you — whyever did you come down to breakfast in your nightclothes?"

"Must have overslept," said the King.

"Funny," the Queen said drowsily. "There were bits of straw in your slippers."

The King said nothing, hoping that she would not next say "Why was that?" But then he heard a small snore and he settled down thankfully. Soon his deeper snores accompanied hers.

In her mini-four-poster the Princess Penelope dreamed pleasant dreams. Johnny came into them, but they were mostly about her pig. In them Lollipop did all sorts of fantastic things that she, Penelope, had taught her to do, like playing the piano and walking on her hind legs and sitting up at the table with a napkin around her neck.

In the stall, on a mattress made of sacks stuffed with straw, Johnny Skinner's dreams were also pleasant ones. Penelope appeared in them, but they were mostly about Lollipop. In one of them she was carefully using her snout to turn over the earth between the rose-bushes while the Queen watched approvingly, saying, "*What* a good pig!"

Beside Johnny, deep in the straw, Lollipop, full-stomached, slept dreamlessly.

Next morning Johnny was summoned to the Palace again. The King was in his study and the Princess was also there. They looked rather pleased with themselves, Johnny thought, as though they were sharing a secret.

"Sit down, Johnny my boy," said the King, and then, "Go on, Penelope, tell him."

"Johnny," said the Princess, "we want you to bring Lollipop to the Royal Gardens after lunch today."

"Does your mother know?" asked Johnny.

"No, and she won't be back till teatime because she's going out this afternoon."

"To a flower show," said the King. "She has entered a bunch of Ethelwynne's Beautifuls in the Hybrid Tea Class."

"And if she wins," said the Princess, "she'll be in such a good mood that perhaps she won't mind about my pig being in the garden, especially if Lollipop has done useful things among the roses. If she doesn't mind her in the garden, maybe she won't mind her in the Palace."

"Bring the pig in through the gates at the bottom of the Royal Gardens, Johnny," said the King, "and then if things don't go right, you can slip out again the same way."

Johnny thought for a minute.

"But suppose things do go right, sir," he said. "Might it be a good idea to have the pig flap ready? The Royal carpenters could make a new door with the flap in it, but leave the old door where it is. Then, if things go according to plan, they could quickly hang the new door and we could demonstrate the whole thing, doormat and all, to the Queen. What d'you think, sir?"

"I think," said the King, "that you may be one step nearer to your dukedom."

So it was that on that very afternoon the King and the Princess and Johnny and Lollipop all met beside the Queen's rose garden. Beside the old door that led out from the Palace into the Royal Gardens a footman stood waiting, with orders to report the Queen's return. Concealed behind some curtains, the Royal carpenters waited, ready to substitute the new door with the pig flap in it, should a signal come later from the rose garden.

Now came the moment to show what Johnny had been training the pig to do in an old patch of rough ground within the Royal Mews. He led her into the rose garden and gave the command "Rootle." At this the pig put her head down and with her snout began to grub up the soil between the rosebushes, turning it all over, burying the weeds, and sifting through the earth to till the soil.

She worked her way methodically around and around the circular rose garden, being careful not to disturb the bushes, until the whole large expanse had been thoroughly cultivated, far more thoroughly than any human gardener could have done.

When Lollipop had finished, she stood looking up at the three watchers, who with one voice cried, "*What* a good pig!"

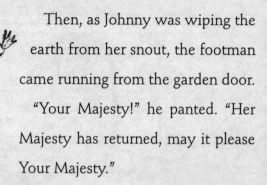

Then, as Johnny was wiping the earth from her snout, the footman came running from the garden door.

"Your Majesty!" he panted. "Her Majesty has returned, may it please Your Majesty."

"Right," said the King. "Now you keep your eye on me, my good man, and if — and only if — I hold both arms up as if I were stretching, you understand, you tell those carpenters to swap the doors."

"Quick, Johnny," said the Princess. "Get Lollipop out of sight. Hide behind that hedge. Don't come out unless I call you."

Then she and her father waited anxiously for the Queen to emerge.

When she did, they saw at once that she wore, pinned upon her dress, one small and one large red rosette.

"Guess what!" she cried happily as she hurried towards them. "I won!"

"What did you win, Eth?" asked the King.

"First Prize in the Hybrid Tea Class!" said the Queen.

"But you've got two rosettes, Mommy," said the Princess.

"Yes!" cried the Queen. "Because my Ethelwynne's Beautifuls won Best in Show!" and she broke into a little dance of joy.

Then she saw her rose bed.

"Oh!" she cried. "How very professionally my rose garden has been dug and weeded!"

"Hasn't it just!" said the King, and "Johnny!" called the Princess, and Johnny Skinner appeared from behind the hedge, followed by Lollipop.

"Whatever is that pig doing here?" said the Queen.

"She's been cultivating your rose garden, ma'am," said Johnny. "Haven't you, Lollipop?" And the pig gave her "Yes" grunt.

"She did it all, Mommy," said the Princess. "She did it all, by herself."

Then she said "Come, Lollipop," and the pig came to her, and "Sit," and the pig sat, gazing up into the Queen's face with bright eyes.

The Queen, staring into those eyes, fringed with long white lashes and shining with intelligence, saw someone not so very different from herself looking back at her.

"Did you really?" said the Queen to Lollipop. "Do it all? By yourself?"

In reply there came a quick, high-pitched grunt.

"*What* a good pig," said Queen Ethelwynne softly. "She must be tired after all that work, and thirsty too. She had better come in to tea." And the King held both his arms up as if he were stretching.

I'll give the boy a job

CHAPTER ELEVEN

"Come along in then, all of you," said the Queen.

But Johnny could see that they needed to play for time — the carpenters had not yet completed the exchange of doors.

"Excuse me, ma'am," he said to the Queen. "Lollipop may need to make herself comfortable before we go indoors."

"Oh, let me tell her, Johnny!" cried the Princess. "I haven't got any horse biscuits on me, but she did sit when I told her to just now. Let me try, can I?"

Johnny nodded, and with that Penelope said to Lollipop (in a bright, encouraging voice), "Busy! Good pig, busy!"

As the Queen watched in amazement, the pig marched back into the center of the rose garden and deposited a generous supply of pig dung at the foot of a fine floribunda.

"Just the stuff for growing prize roses, ma'am," said Johnny quietly to the Queen.

"She did it!" cried the Princess. "She did it when I told her to, Johnny! Did you see, Mommy? Did you see, Daddy? It isn't only Johnny she obeys, it's me too!" And confidently she called "Come, Lollipop" and Lollipop came, and then "Heel!" and Lollipop walked sedately to heel beside the Princess, followed by the King and Johnny and a mystified Queen.

Even more mystified was she when they reached the Palace's garden door, for she could see how different it now looked.

"What is that, in the door?" she asked.

"It's a pig flap, Mommy," said the Princess. "It's an invention of Johnny's. Lollipop will be able to go in and out as she likes."

"But her feet . . ." said the Queen, looking at the pig's muddy trotters.

"Don't worry, ma'am," said Johnny. "If you will all go inside, you'll see."

So the Royal Family all went in through the new

garden door while Johnny kept Lollipop sitting beside him outside.

Once they had closed the door behind them, Johnny called "Right" and, from inside, the Princess called "Come, Lollipop" and the pig pushed open the pig flap with her snout and entered.

"Wipe your feet," commanded the Princess, and then her pig carefully wiped her trotters, one after another, on the doormat.

How they praised the Princess's pig, and how they laughed when the pig flap swung open again and through it, on hands and knees and grunting loudly, came Johnny Skinner, grinning all over his face.

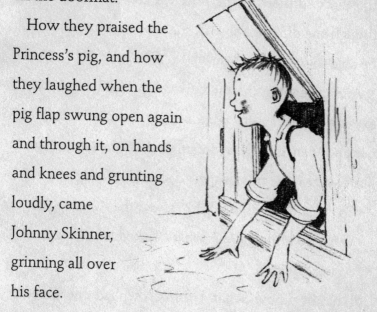

After that, everything went swimmingly. As they made their way through the Palace, Lollipop, walking close at heel beside the Princess, made a series of strange little noises, snuffles, chuckles, and chortles, as she looked around her in wonder at all the rich furnishings, at the ornaments of gold and silver, at the portraits of the King's ancestors looking down at her from the tapestried walls, and felt beneath her trotters the thick softness of the priceless carpets upon which, though she did not know it, she would in future always be able to walk.

And at teatime the pig behaved perfectly. She didn't exactly sit up at the table with a napkin around her neck as Penelope had dreamed, but she ate toasted, buttered teacake from a silver dish as delicately as a lady.

"So what d'you think, Eth?" asked the King.

"What do I think about what?" asked the Queen.

"About Lollipop."

"I hardly know what I think," replied the Queen,

fingering the two red rosettes she wore. "Today has been so extraordinary. But Penelope's pig is certainly a most remarkable animal."

"With a most remarkable trainer by the name of Johnny Skinner," said the King.

"And a most remarkable owner," cried the Princess, "who is now going to keep her pet pig in the Palace, but only, of course, if her mother says that she can."

"Please, Mommy?"

Johnny and the King both looked at the Princess and each thought, What a cunning little minx!

The Queen looked at her daughter and thought how she had changed. Gone were the sulks and the shouting and the selfishness, and instead here was this happy, jolly little girl. How had it happened? It must be something to do with that boy.

"Can I, Mommy?" the Princess said again. "Can I keep her here?"

The Queen fed another teacake to the pig.

"We'll see," she said.

King and Princess looked at one another and father winked at daughter. The battle was won, they knew, but each was thinking, What about Johnny?

"What about Johnny, Eth?" said King Theophilus.

"What about him?"

"Well, he can't spend the rest of his life in a stall, not after all he's done for us, in the way of helping Penelope — with her pig, I mean."

It *is* something to do with that boy, thought Queen Ethelwynne, and just as though she could read that thought, Lollipop turned to the Queen and made her high-pitched "Yes" grunt.

I thought as much, said the Queen to herself. It's he who has made Penelope so much more reasonable. And my roses — he's so good on roses. And that pig — cultivator and dung spreader rolled into one. I'll give the boy a job.

"Well?" said the King.

"Well?" said the Princess.

"Well," said the Queen, "I could do with some help in the garden. And there's a cottage vacant. It's very small, but cozy. How would you like to be my under-gardener, Johnny?"

Lady Lollipop!

CHAPTER TWELVE

The news
traveled fast
in the Palace, and
soon everyone, from the Lord High Chamberlain to the
smallest scullery boy, knew that Princess Penelope's pet
was now a palace pig, sleeping on a sheepskin rug at the
foot of her mistress's mini-four-poster and, should the
need arise, making her way down the Grand Staircase,
out through the pig flap, and on to the rose bed.

They knew also that the Queen had a new under-
gardener with whom she talked endlessly about

flower beds and borders, and lawns and lily-ponds, and, especially, about roses.

And all of them saw how much happier the Royal Family was, now that the Princess was no longer a spoiled brat, but a happy pig keeper.

One evening, a lovely summer's evening, the King and the Queen were sitting out in the gardens, watching their daughter training her pig, when they saw Johnny come out of his little cottage beyond the vegetable patch.

"Penelope!" they heard him call. "Where are you, Penelope?"

"Did you hear that, Theo?" said the Queen. "Isn't it a bit much that Johnny Skinner, a commoner, should address the Princess by name?"

"I shouldn't worry, Eth," the King said. "I'm going to make him a duke."

"Honestly, Theo," said the Queen, laughing. "Next thing, you'll be ennobling the pig!"

"I shall," said the King, as they sat and watched their daughter and her pig running to meet the boy who had been the owner of one and was the playmate of the other. "I *shall* be making her a lady. **Lady Lollipop!**"

Other books by Dick King-Smith

Babe: The Gallant Pig

Sophie's Snail

Sophie's Tom

Sophie Hits Six

Sophie in the Saddle

Sophie Is Seven

Sophie's Lucky

All Pigs Are Beautiful

I Love Guinea Pigs

Dick King-Smith's Animal Friends